1

THE PAINTED DESERT

A Young Adult Novel

By Susan Smith Nash

Copyright Page

THE PAINTED DESERT

A Young Adult Novel

Copyright © 2025 by Susan Smith Nash

First Edition

ISBN: 978-1-945784-17-0 -- Paperback

ISBN: 978-1-945784-18-7 -- E-Book

Printed in the United States of America

For more information about the author and future works, visit:

http:///www.texturepress.org

TABLE OF CONTENTS

CHAPTER ONE

I LIVE ACROSS THE STREET and down one from Kithie Wexthrall -- the girl everyone knows after she got in trouble at school for being mistakenly accused of being a cyberbully.

What actually happened was this: her little brother Gus had shared a video of her where she was doing a mocking version of a dance that the cheer team had made popular on TikTok. "Look at me! I'm AVZM!" read the caption. They were not amused. They were awesome (AVZM), and indisputably so. Who was Kithie Wexthrall to mock them?

It was an accident, and Kithie was just messing aroung. But by then it was too late. The story had already spread through social media. "Kithie Wexthrall thinks she is AVZM (LOL)" It was not pleasant for anyone.

I am sure Kithie has seen me -- after all, I'm her neighbor -- but she probably doesn't know my name. I'm a lot younger. I'm nine. She's fourteen or fifteen.

Kithie is tall for her age, with sharp cheekbones that make her look older than she is, especially when she pulls her dark brown hair back in a severe ponytail. Her eyes are the color of storm clouds, and they have this way of looking right through you, like she's seeing something you can't. She wears oversized black hoodies that swallow her thin frame, and she walks with her shoulders hunched forward, as if she's carrying an invisible weight. The kids at school whisper that she's dangerous, but I think she just looks tired. Bone-deep tired from carrying the shame of being mocked. Never mind that it looked like she was mocking first. She was just having fun and then Gus had to go and post it to TikTok. Oops.

I'm even younger than Gus -- the one everyone considers the computer prodigy. He is, but I'm better. But, no one knows it. No one knows my name. I like it that way. It is good to be invisible.

Gus is small for eleven, with messy red curls that stick up no matter what he does to them, and freckles scattered across his pale face like constellation maps. He has these bright green eyes that light up when he talks about coding or when he's explaining some new algorithm he's discovered. His fingers are always moving, either typing on his phone or tapping out invisible keyboards on his thighs. He says he's sick of typing and also voice to text, so he wants to train his phone to decode his gestures. He wears the same three graphic t-shirts in rotation -- one with binary code that spells out "Hello World," another with a pixelated lightning bolt and blast with the words "Charged Creeper," and a faded blue one that just says "404: Social Skills Not Found."

Especially if you're little, you're alone, and you are stuck with always wanting what you can't have.

Someone asked me once what it was that I wanted. "What do you want? What IS IT that you want?" That was the way they phrased it, so I knew they really didn't care at all what I wanted -- they just wanted to express their anger and dissatisfaction with my unwillingness to be perky, happy, and to wear a tiara and a tutu which, by the way, would NEVER happen.

I'm the runt of the ballet class whose mom had to pull her out from under the bed and manhandle her into the car to get her to go to Madame Keeling's Dance Academy in the little brick office building on Main Street.

Unlike the other girls in my ballet class -- all pink tutus and sparkly hair ribbons and mothers who beam with pride from the observation window -- I look like I belong in a different century. My hair is the color of wheat fields in autumn, long and straight, and I usually wear it in two tight braids that reach halfway down my back. My eyes are blue-gray, like morning fog, and my face is all sharp angles -- pointed chin, high cheekbones, serious mouth that rarely smiles. I'm small for nine, thin as a rail, with arms and legs that seem too long for my body. When I dance, though, everything fits together. When I dance, I'm not awkward anymore.

It mattered not at all to me that Madame Keeling had tears in her eyes -- real tears, not crocodile tears -- after our rehearsals.

I started taking classes when I was four because my mom saw me trying to be Mikhail Baryshnikov (Mishka for me), and I'd play the same recording of him over and over and over... I loved the way he could do split leaps and endless, clockwork-like pirouettes.

I know we're talking in generalities and universals, but I'd like to move to the specific right now. I'd like to talk to you about dance, and to help you understand why I did not want to wear the lovely Degas-inspired long-skirted tutu, nor did I want to don a tiara of any kind -- rhinestone, lace, feathers, or any combination of the above.

Yes, I love to dance. I love the stories and the characters -- black swans, rat kings, and mad dollmakers...

Don't make me cry. Please.

Or, if I do, just look the other way and hear me out. I never cry, but I suddenly feel strangely emotional -- I'm not used to being able to talk to anyone. My heart is gentle, but it's also strong and passionate. No one knows this, and I'm not used to saying things with words. You've probably already guessed that I say things with the way I move, the way I throw my arms and legs out, and form my body into hard and painful yet glorious moves and gestures.

You read the language of my heart, and I cheerfully express it to you.

But of course it's not so easy.

I can't tell you why I was so afraid to go to dance class, especially since I loved to dance, and I could do so many of the things I saw Mishka do. I could do a split leap with a perfect line -- my legs extended and my back arched and sweet. I could do perfect "pas des chats" followed by lovely arabesques and lyrical port-a-bras... okay, I'm nine years old and not 20-something, but I can watch moves that amaze me, and I can try to do them myself, right?

But, back to my mom having to drag me out from under the bed to take me to dance class. Somehow it hurt me to go to there. I can't really explain it, except to say that being in the class with the other girls, and their mothers watching their little darlings take their dance lessons, took the sweetness and the light out of it.

Funny, on a physical level, the enforced mediocrity also took away the pain, the drama, and the soaring highs. It sickened me that during class I could not be myself. I had to hide myself, and keep myself under wraps. I felt like a dog with a muzzle. I had to be polite, quiet, dull, and bland. But I did not want to be.

From the very beginning -- at 4 years of age, I wanted to soar, to fly, to twirl, and to meet my maker in the transcendent heavens that are Dance. I have always been oblivious to pain when I'm in pursuit of my passion. I just want to take that leap that connects me to an amazing, glorious, happy place -- the joy of dance. And -- when I'm in my state of exultation and soaring unity, I don't want people to stare, laugh, or make me feel stupid.

But, invariably, they did, and so I hid under the bed.

I'm 9 years old now, and I'll tell you a secret. Please don't tell anyone else.

Yes, I go to Madame Keeling's still. But my secret is in my bedroom and in the big empty garage in the house that's been for sale for 2 years now, and will probably be on the market for another 2 years (or 200 according to my mom).

It's the place where I take my music and my heart, and I work -- joyously and with the infinitude that is my mind -- to perfect all the things I see the great dancers do.

Thanks to my mom, I have an iPad and a great data plan, so I can stream the videos I so love... and thanks to my dad, who lives in somewhere in South America now, but feels guilty enough to send me $500 a month, I have been able to buy plexiglass mirrors I hide in a closet, but install against the main wall of the inside of the oversized three-car garage. I also have a playlist with the music that makes me soar; and to which I've sketched out the kind of choreography that Mishka made come alive....

I wish you could watch me dance in that garage, with me in headphones watching myself in the mirrors, wishing I had a partner who could pull, push, spin, twist, stretch, and clench herself into control with me...

Perhaps the truth is the truth. You are my partner.

I just wish I knew who you were.

In the meantime, I'll share a very well-kept secret with you. Do you remember Kithie's computer genius brother, Gus, age 10? Well, he's now 11, and he's still quite good.

But, I'm better. I'm 9 years old, and I'm much, much better at computers than he is.

I think it's because he's always tried to make money with his skills -- ringtones, goofy apps, whatever.

I'm a purist. I like staying behind the scenes. No one has any idea.

So. Hang on. Hang in there. We're in for a rocky ride, but you'll never regret the decision to take me on, and to go with me.

I love you very much.

CHAPTER TWO

The letter I'll never send.

Dear Dad.

Dear Daddy.

I hate you.

Okay. That's too strong.

But I am really mad at you. And I love you. I love you desperately, painfully, longingly -- just the way you'd expect a little girl to love her Daddy -- the Daddy who's never there, who never sees her glorious moments, her graceful, athletic dance moves that make you realize you're a human being of flesh and blood and mind and passion -- the kind of person who hangs back a bit before plunging into that space where all bets are off, and you'll either soar to the heavens or you'll fall hard and fast onto the ugly black fundament of death-ridden Planet Earth.

I miss you. I need you. But, you've already forgotten who I am.

Okay. I know I'm being too hard on you. Mom explained to me that you do love me. After all, your Child Support Checks (I'm capitalizing them because that's the way Mom talks about them) arrive like clockwork. So yes. You love me. You provide me with food, with sustenance, with the funds necessary to keep me in a good private school and the latest, best laptop and mobile devices.

I have not told anyone this, and I probably never will.

My father is a shadow in my memory now, someone I piece together from old photographs and Mom's bitter comments after she's had margaritas with her friends on Girls Night Out. In the pictures, he's tall and lean with dark hair that curls at the edges, and he has my same blue-gray eyes. He's always smiling in those photos, his arm around Mom's waist, looking like he belongs in a cologne advertisement. But memories can lie. People can pretend to be happy when the camera clicks.

Dear Dad,

I remembered you used to like white cats, and well, there was white cat sneaking around in the yellow rose bushes that Mom planted last year, and which are going a bit crazy with roses this year -- probably because your gardener Pablito (from Aguascalientes, Mexico, in case you're curious, which I suspect you're not) knows just how to baby the roses...

Anyway .. oh Daddy, please understand .. please talk to me about this ... I need to talk to someone ..

I saw an old white cat and it seemed it was going to hurt the bushes. I got the cat to come up to me by acting as though I was really a cat-lover, a chat-o-phile (don't you love my French! Thank ballet 7 days a week..!) .. but I was a liar, a dissembler, a monster.

The white cat came up to me. It meowed and when it did so, I instantly hated it. It seemed muscular and independent -- it was obviously a male cat, and it had an ugly smell. All I could think of at that moment, my Father Dearest, was that you were gone, gone, gone... and you were laughing, laughing, laughing...

So, I caught the big, white, trusting cat and wanted to smack that jowly, snarky cat across his bloated white face. I trembled with emotion and I held him against my chest. That magnificent sad white dodgy old cat did not try to scratch me. He did not try to bite me.

He ran away.

He then stood at the end of the flowerbed and looked at me with unblinking eyes.

He looked glad he had gotten away. He could sense that I wanted to hold him tight and never let him go.

He turned his face to me, opened his eyes, and then his mouth. He meowed. Then he meowed again.

MieeRaowwww!! Meeeeeooooww!! Roauw!

At the time, I thought it was stupid, nonsensical mewling ... now I realize he was saying something to me about giving up and just letting go. He read my pain.

Well, Daddy. I'm sorry. I can't make the pain go away.

Whatever. (sigh)

Daddy, where are you?

I love you.

Your daughter,

Marie Elise (Lulu)

CHAPTER THREE

One thing I hate about neighbors (or being someone's neighbor) is that you're eventually going to know more about them than you want to, and it gets awkward. It can even be embarrassing. You start to see their patterns.

When Kithie's mom is between voice-acting contracts and has a lot of time on her hands, she starts planting a lot of flowers in her front yard, and taking their dog on long walks wearing attention-getting outfits. My mom says it's pretty clear she's missed her calling and should design outfits for Anime Cosplay events. Mom says it in a totally deprecatory manner and sort of sniff-laughs at the end of the sentence. I don't know why that is considered a negative. I love costumes, whether for ballet or for role-playing. My favorites are Sailor Moon (so cute!), Ruby Rose, Demon Slayer, and, of course, Harley Quinn. If Kithie's mom actually wanted to design some outfits, I'd like to work with her. It would be amazing.

Kithie's mom, Elena, used to be beautiful in that specific way that child stars are beautiful -- all big eyes and perfect features and practiced smiles. She was the cute little girl vampire, Little Anna, in Family Plot, a comedy series that featured a family of vampires. She still receives checks for residuals and is invited to nostalgia events. Now, at forty-something, she's still striking, but in a brittle way. Her blonde hair is always perfectly styled, her makeup never smudged, her clothes showing real creativity in the way she combines colors, patterns, footwear, and accessories. He voice is smooth, low, and incredibly expressive. My mom calls it mellifluous and always comments on how much she likes it. She makes a fashion statement every time she walks the dog. It's like she's still performing for an audience that stopped watching years ago. It's sad, but I really enjoy seeing what she'll put together.

When you're in the clutches of memories of a glorious past, you become a prisoner to raw longings for what you know you can't have -- what just out of reach -- all the while not knowing exactly what it is that you want. I think that's what's going on with Kithie's mom. It's not easy to be a former child star, and even if you get voice acting lessons, you're still not anything like the star you were as a kid.

I look at Kithie's mom at those times and I see her as a victim -- sad and embarrassing at times. My mom looks away and pretends that nothing is out of ordinary, and that she won't yield to commenting when the outfits are extremely extravagant.

What I hate about being a neighbor is that you see other neighbors taking the bait.

There was a guy down the street who was renting the garage apartment of old Mr. Turabian. I think he was probably a graduate student or perhaps caught in the transition zone of an ugly breakup or a job relocation. He seemed nice enough -- kind of quiet, distant, slightly lacking people skills. He's just the sort of guy who is easily played by someone needing a lot of attention, but who can't give anything back.

A few years ago we had a problem with mice. My mom blames our dog and the fact he liked to eat IAMS dry dog food which came in a bag that always split open. "It draws mice!" she said. She did not consider putting the food into a plastic bin or a big Tupperware bowl with a self-sealing lid. No, my mom just got mad when the mice invaded the house. To take care of the problem, she came home with an armload of glue-traps -- the cruelest pest extermination methods known to humankind (in my opinion). They are little plastic platters with inch-deep tacky, slippery glue that smells like peanut butter or whatever it is that rats can't resist.

Anyway, I saw how it works. The mice were drawn to the scent of peanut butter, and they waded into the glue, hoping to have a moment of sweet unity with their favorite food.

But, it was not to be.

Once they stuck their little snouts into what they thought would be hot, satisfying sweetness, they were lost. They suffocated in the glue. The word, "suffocated" does not really capture the details of what happened.

I couldn't watch, and then I couldn't stop watching.

It still traumatizes me just to recall the way the little things writhed and twisted in the glue.

I wanted to pull the mice out of the glue, but my mom refused to let me touch them. "You'll get a disease!" So all I could do was watch -- watch them slowly die -- and I just felt so, so sad that they paid such a high, terrible price for their love of peanut-y, crunchy satisfaction, and a moment when they could live without being dogged by some sort of existential hunger.

All I can say is that I'm still sad about what I saw.

And, oh yes, my sad, hungry neighbor -- Mr. Turabian's tenant -- and my smooth, sweet, peanut-scented neighbor, Kithie's mom -- well, what can I say? Yes. It was a glue trap, pure and simple.

Sometimes I hate being a neighbor.

Sometimes I see her standing at her kitchen window at night, just staring out at the street with this empty expression, like she's waiting for someone who's never going to come.

CHAPTER FOUR

I'm going to tell you something that you probably will not want to hear.

I have not been a good girl. I have not been what you think I should be. I've done things I should not do.

If only I had a way to cut myself off at the pass -- intervene, swoop in, extend my huge eagle talon and grab myself up from this sinful rabble, well, yes, I'd be much better.

But I don't know how to do that, and you're not helping me. You, yes, you. You, the entity I call my higher power, my unity-being, my love, in a word, God.

If this were the 1950s, I'd be watching the neighbor kids playing with big, wooden kitchen matches in a dry wheat field, and I'd be breathing deep that sulfur-smell as I tackled the little boy and grabbed the matches from his hand. "What are you trying to do? Build your own Hell?" In my mind, I would see ignited air that crackles and sparks with snapping embers and hear the lung-sizzle of super-heated gases.

Yesterday, I found another one. He was thin and his coat had little tears. His left ear was ragged and chewed, and I could tell he was a little scrappy streetfighter who just couldn't go on any more. He was easy to lure into my box.

If this were the 1970s, I'd be out there in the streets shouting about wars and peace, death and delivery, rights and equality, and I'd be the very best sloganeer you could possibly imagine because each hand-lettered sign, each jingoistic ditty shouted at the top of my lungs would seem to offer absolution, at least in the mental space in which I'm charging myself to another plane of existence. I would be trying to change the world. I'd give it all up after Watergate, though.

Yesterday was disconcerting. The little cat I found did not move at all while I carried him in the tight little Igloo plastic container. I worried that he had suffocated, but he wasn't suffocating at all, he just looked up at me with big golden eyes.

If this were the late 1990s, I'd be starting a Y2K cult and, in the face of impending apocalypse, I would talk about the need to efface one's identity. "You've got to subjugate individual self," I'd say, and I'd reinforce the belief that we should never create art with a human face.

My mom likes to brag that we've got the biggest, coolest house on the block. I have never cared, except I do like exploring the attic and there is a large, empty basement. My mom never goes there because the stairs are rickety and the handrail is shaky. Her knees are bad and she has a tough time because of her size. Too bad.

If this were the early 2000s, I'd use all the tools at my disposal to pioneer flash mobs, and I'd work really, really hard at getting people to meet at a certain time and place, and but instead of singing show tunes or wearing pink ribbons to show solidarity in the fight against breast cancer, I'd ask everyone to wear something they've made themselves. DIY! Yes, that's it. Do it yourself.

I brought my little cat downstairs. "Don't go anywhere," I whispered, then locked the door.

But now is now, and I don't know what to do. You know how it goes. You start doing something and it seems innocent enough -- even noble. But before you know it, it's turned into something you can't control.

Water. Food. Litter box.

It's not my fault. I'm not the one doing the cat-dumping at the arched stone bridge at the creek.

CHAPTER FIVE

Lulu decided it was time to stop playing the ignorant "gaijan" with the new sushi place that wasn't so new any more.

"Why did you name your restaurant Sushi Neko?" asked the thin but muscular little girl with blonde braids that hung down her back.

"It is a name that has been in our family for a long time," said the short, spiky-haired guy who brought out the take-out order.

"Which name? Sushi or Neko?" asked the little girl.

The small, thin girl dressed in a bright pink tennis dress that was half a size too large for her walked up the steps to the restaurant, pulled a sheaf of papers out of her backpack and slammed them down on the To Go / Take Out counter.

Her blonde braids swayed back and forth as she bobbed her head. The bright yellow terry headband, and the bright pink bows at the end of her braids made it appear butterflies were getting ready to fly around the sun, or an angel's halo. Her heart-shaped face turned up, and her blue eyes suggested the sky.

"Hi there, cutie. What do you have there?" A guy in his late 30s dressed in a white apron wearing a chef's hat walked up to her. "Are you selling Girl Scout cookies? I'll take a couple of boxes."

"No, sir. This is something very different," said the girl. Her face was tense, her voice tight. "These are papers -- a court injunction that I'm going to get signed by a judge. It's about your restaurant."

"Is someone waiting for you in the car? Did they put you up to this? You're not a process server, are you?" He looked nervous. Lulu noticed his body art was a bit faded. She had no idea what prison tats looked like, but she suddenly wondered.

"It's a cease and desist order. It's all about shutting you down," she said. She paused, took a big breath, and continued. "You know there's no reason in the world for you to call yourselves NEKO SUSHI. It's bad. Very bad. You are making people think bad things about what might be in your sushi."

"What? Fish? Eel? Yellowfin?" said the man, clearly mystified. "It's what people love. And, it's always fresh." The wooden restaurant door creaked open again and a young woman came in to order sushi to go. The vibration of the floor made the gigantic beckoning cat, the "maneki neko" wave his paw up and down like a mellow metronome. Clearly the owners liked the maneki neko's size and the possibility that he could attract extremely good luck.

Their luck was about to change if they did not change, thought Lulu.

"You know the name of your restaurant --?" she asked.

"Sure. Neko Sushi."

"Don't you know what that means?" she asked. The woman behind her looked impatient.

"Is this where I should order? I'm sort of in a hurry," she said. She had dark red streaks in her short brunette hair and her nose had two piercings.

The man reached out his hand so the woman could give him her order. She handed it to him.

"We'll get after this right away."

Lulu took another deep breath and looked at the man, then looked at the customer.

"This is a court injunction that states that if you do not change the name of your restaurant, you must shut down," she said.

"Huh? What's wrong with Neko Sushi?" asked the employee. The customer stopped, typed something into her iPhone, then started laughing.

"Haha -- your restaurant name means CAT SUSHI and it's right down the street from "Cat Dump Bridge"!" She laughed.

Lulu looked at her imploringly. "So you get it, right? It sounds bad. I just want them to change their name to something like HAPPY CAT SUSHI or LUCKY CAT SUSHI or MANEKI NEKO SUSHI and then to have a picture of a big beckoning good luck happy cat on all the advertising and the logo. I don't want anyone to think bad thoughts."

"You'll have to talk to the owner," he said. "I get it, but I can't do anything."

The customer held out her hand to Lulu.

"My name is Delia, and I would be happy to help. I know Hichiro pretty well, and I think he would be happy to do so. What do you have there? Do you mind if I take a look?"

After shaking Delia's hand, Lulu handed her the papers. "Call me Lulu. These are just copies. I can print more. They're not signed yet."

Delia moved her long bangs out of her face. Her dark purple lipstick contrasted with her pale foundation. She was wearing purple and black.

"I'll get started on your order," said the cook, looking relieved to get away from the two females.

"Lulu. I like the way you think. Yes, I think we can do something."

CHAPTER SIX

"Do you mind if I ask you a few questions?" asked the thin little girl with long braids and a serious expression on her face.

The man wearing a button-down shirt, khaki slacks, and Johnston & Murphy shoes seemed surprised that she asked him a question.

"Sure, shoot," he said. "You're a spunky little thing, aren't you?"

"You needn't patronize me," she said. "I have to look out for my mother's interests, given that she won't, or, well, in more realistic terms, can't."

"Okay. You've got me there. But, you don't have to worry. I think your mother's pretty special, and I want to spend some time with her." He paused when he saw the scowl on her face. "I will add, though, I think it's pretty standard practice for the child to resent any and all interlopers."

The thin little girl pulled out a small spiral notebook and a small tablet computer.

"Go ahead. I don't much care," she said. "Oh, and please call me Lulu," she said. She had decided to distance herself from her name, Marie Elise. That would be the name she would save to use with her father.

"Why?" he asked. "Who is Lulu? I have to say you don't look much like a Lulu to me. But, I have never met anyone named Lulu. Wasn't that a comic book character."

"No. But you're close. Fictive constructs do not seem to have the same narrative and epistemological constraints as historical figures."

"How old are you?"

"I will be 10 in January," she said. "I am glad we can talk. And, I'm glad you seem open. I won't ask you the toughest of the questions I have on my mind.

We can pretend ... or at least I can pretend... to be objective. I'll tell you right now, though, I'm not. I'm on to you, and I don't like the way you act. I'm not blaming you, though. You know what you want and you think you know how to get it."

"Okay, Lulu. But, I'd like to hear your tough questions, too."

She felt a wave of relief. It felt good to go by the name of Lulu. Did he recognize the allusion to Gustave Flaubert's "Un Coeur Simple," and Lulu, the parrot?

"My mom acts as though she believes you really care about her. She is not as stupid as you think."

"Why is that?"

"She's fat and old. That makes her easy."

"Lulu, you're nine years old. Anyone over 14 is going to seem old. And, you're a rail-thin dancer-type little girl. I don't know what you consider "fat" but your mom's not that," he said. He leaned back in his chair and crossed his arms across his chest.

The thin, little girl leaned toward him. Her braids moved back and forth like pendulums.

"I know my mother. She's not young and pretty -- at least not now. When she was in her teens and early twenties, she looked just like some of the movie stars of that time, so I know that her life must have been amazing. Her life is not that now, though, and I know she would like nothing better than to travel back in time 20 years and stay forever fresh, young, and pretty."

"Forever young? Is that what you're saying? I don't like that in a woman. I prefer intelligence," he said.

"My mom makes me sad. She has to pay to play. Doesn't she get it? I am sorry to be the one to tell her, but at her point in life, it's all about 'pay to play,'" she said.

"Where on earth do you get your ideas?" he asked. "It's like watching a combination of a self-help women's talk show and crime drama."

The little girl looked him full in the eyes, and he noticed they were full of tears.

"Does it help that she's worth a lot of money, but she won't let anyone know? She inherited the house, but it's not what has made her wealthy. In fact, the house has cost her a lot. She's worth a lot of money because of the companies she helped turn around. She could still do that, but something happened and she has a broken wing."

The little girl wiped tears from her eyes.

"She needs a compassionate, strong companion -- not an opportunist," she said.

"Okay. So there's a way I'll agree with you. My mom is vulnerable. Not stupid in the way that we like to think of people being vulnerable, but in the way that she superimposes her own version of reality over what really exists. Usually it doesn't matter. But, in the case of her feelings for you, it does matter. She sees too much sorrow and suffering in you and she wants to take away your pain. But, to do so means that she is humiliated by you, and I just won't stand for it."

"Did someone script this for you? Did your dad put you up to this?"

"My dad died when I was three," she said. It was not true, but if the truth ever came out, she'd sort it out later.

"I did not know that, but ... well... so where did this come from?"

"You're not nice."

"I'm nicer than you think .. I am telling you the truth about the way the world works. If you don't like it, don't worry -- the world offers an option -- actually, many options.... If you can't do what you want, you can find all sorts of "no fault" death opportunities..."

"You see, sir, this is why I don't trust you. What are you talking about? Are you hinting that you might hurt my mother? Kill her, even? Make it look like an accident?"

"No and yes. I'm intrigued by your mind, so I'm deliberately throwing you cues and clues that are painfully provocative," he said. "They should tell you something. Look within. Understand yourself and when your buttons are being pushed, when you're being played and your emotions triggered."

"My mom does not see you when she talks to you. She sees her own past, and the moments of wonder and joy that shaped and transformed her at a particular time in her life. You're conveniently positioned to be the surface upon which she projects her memories, and ... more importantly, her nostalgia. It's really not right of you to take advantage of her."

"But I truly care about her," he said.

"You know that's false. Look within. Look at your own experience. You know how people react to you. She is kind. She is telling you you're wonderful and great."

"You think I'm not?"

"I think you're kind of uninteresting. But, what do I know? I'm a kid," she said.

"You're brilliant."

"Thank you."

"You're welcome."

"And I don't know what else to say, but I have to reiterate that I can't stand by and watch you make her pay you for your company."

"Lulu, your mom is beautiful. And, isn't it time for you to do something else? Homework? Tennis? Bedtime?"

"Haha. I'm amused," said Lulu. "I'm out of here, though. See you, sir."

He watched the serious little girl walk quickly down the street, her steps breaking into a skip every quarter block or so. He shook his head in disbelief. What was that all about? He secretly looked forward to the next round.

CHAPTER SEVEN

I've wanted to do this for as long as I can remember. I could never bring it up to my mother, though. She would not understand.

The basement is perfect. There are at least two large rooms I can soundproof. There is plenty of room for me to put carpeted poles, ramps, and ledges -- perfect for climbing and clawing. There are little air vents at the top and a fan that brings in fresh air from little windows behind the rosebushes.

I don't know why, but people seem to like to dump kittens off the bridge that's next to the small park and azalea garden down the street from our house.

When my mom's dad died, she inherited this house. She said she always hated it because it has violent spirit. In my opinion, the only violent spirit is the one that's within her that pushes her to eat too much, drink too much, take pain pills... Sure, for awhile she feels no pain, but then it's all pain, all the time.

Then there's that violent hatred toward herself and toward all those who she thinks can see past the surface and into her inner self. All pain, all the time.

I see it. I have always seen it. I also feel it. I feel her waves of resentment and hatred and how she hates me along with the rest of the world. It's confusing because it's not that way all the time. Sometimes she holds me tight and calls me her honey bunny. Usually, though, quickly thereafter, she falls asleep on one of the brocade and silk moiree sofas in cozy room with the gas-converted pot belly stove.

I kind of don't know how / why she is still alive.

But, that's another story.

The kittens are very thin and frightened when I find them. They are too young and foolish to not know that the need to stop mewling if they don't want an opossum or coyote to sneak up and grab them.

The little cries and mews are not at all the same as ones you hear from kittens that are hungry. No, these are terrible, edge of consciousness, edge-of-the-abyss cries -- creatures who know what it is like to feel their mother's warm belly, the soft fur, the body-hot milk filling their mouths and running down their throats. They know the joy of letting their little claws unfurl and sink into their little brothers and sisters as they jockey for the best teat.

From there, they are wrenched, thrown into a bag, then thrown hurled from the bridge, and when they tear themselves out of the soggy, wet, craftpaper second womb, and rebirth themselves it's in a horrible, parallel universe where wet, cold grass substitutes for their mother's soft, warm fur, and thick, gritty mud sticks on their teeth and tongues.

The basement is a special one. It does not smell like mold or dampness. Instead, it has a dry gingerbread smell. I don't really understand it, but I like it. I used to think the gingerbread smell came from a ghost who liked to cook -- a baker? A pastry chef in an elegant patisserie?

I think they used to store ginger root down here. Ginger oil's in the concrete, and when there's a change of weather the scent is pushed out into the room, and I love it.

Barnard, the tallest, fattest kid in fifth grade (probably because he was kept back a year) says he loves it when someone throws a bag of cats off the bridge.

Barnard says one of these days, he's going to find them and bash all their heads in with a rock. He says he'll do that to me first, though. He'll bash my head in first. He can't wait. I deserve it because I'm smart and I make everyone look bad.

The house is big -- it's an amazing Victorian mansion that was built at the time they put a railroad station here, and the town became a major transit point for equipment used in cattle operations, slaughterhouses, wheat farming, and gypsum products. There are a few houses like it down the street, but they're smaller. The other houses were demolished in the 70s, 80s, and 90s, and new houses were built. Kithie's mom bought one of them, and while I like it a lot, it looks pretty out of place -- it is situated in a beautiful wooded, sloped pocket of land and it has a Frank Lloyd Wright "Falling Waters" feeling while my mom preferred the old Victorian. Kind of doesn't make sense given Kithie's mom was a child star in television series about a vampire family that lived in an old Victorian mansion.

Right now, my mom is sorting receipts and writing checks. Soon she will tire of it and will shove pile the receipts into a big plastic hamper she uses as her receipt bin. While she works, she is cutting herself wedges of cheese and thumbing through the book, "Low-Carb / No-Carb Painless Weight Loss." She's wearing a soft green velour warmup top and stretchy workout pants that have pockets for tennis balls. Her hair is pulled back into a messy ponytail.

She puts down the book, the receipts, and picks up her cell phone.

"Todd, do you have time for a lesson today?" she asks the tennis pro at the club.

She fidgets. She has the attention span of a fruit fly, whose only purpose in life is to mate, procreate, and die.

Oh no. It's one of those days. The manic days are infinitely worse than the depressed ones.

CHAPTER EIGHT

You can't sugarcoat it. My mother is not in very good shape.

For the slick guy in the khakis and shiny Johnston & Murphy tasseled loafers to say otherwise is to insult my intelligence by suggesting I can't tell when he's being a callow sycophant.

Yes, he's trying everything in pursuit of my mother. With this huge house, her bad hips and fairly poor mobility, I'm sure she looks like easy pickings.

He'll find out soon enough (as others do as well), that she is, in a word, impossible. Actually, "impossible" was what she was two or three years ago. She's much worse now.

I'm not sure if there's a word for it, and I'm not really ready to describe her day-to-day behavior, or how she responds to male courting (or their attempts).

She does not really bring up my dad, although I know she still loves him. I'm not even sure they're legally divorced, even though she talks about child support and that's the term usually used when there's some sort of divorce decree and a child custody and support order.

Legal documents.

Ah yes.

I like them.

But, my mom's attitude toward them is supreme indifference.

Okay, back to the Don Juan wannabes. The other night on the Turner Classics channel, there was a movie, *The Roman Spring of Mrs. Stone,* based on a novel by Tennessee Williams. It starred Vivien Leigh as an aging movie star who can no longer play the roles she prefers -- Juliet, for example. (There's just no way a 50-something can play a 15-year-old. Better to have a boy play the role!)

Anyway, Mrs. Stone starts keeping a male companion, a syrupy, flattering man, played by Warren Beatty. He's a creepy con artist, and he's playing both Karen Stone and his pimp, a greedy and weird Italian comtessa. During the airing of the movie, the commentator said it was one of Warren Beatty's first roles, and one of Vivien Leigh's last. She was vulnerable. Warren Beatty knew how to push all her buttons. It was really sad.

The commentator did not mention that the plot echoed Tennessee Williams' own life, and what he saw around him -- the fate of an aging queen. I think what pained me most was to see how helplessly self-destructive she became as she tried to face the fact that she had aged and she would never be 15 again -- or 30 or 40, for that matter.

You couldn't sugarcoat it.

I'd like to see a movie where a serial gigolo con artist and a black widow who has murdered at least three or four husbands try to seduce and con each other. I'm sure there's a movie out there in which that happens, and I'm sure Shakespeare has covered a plot that is similar, at least in spirit. It's a contest but they don't realize it. They're just focused on their own goal -- to hasten death and reap the spoils (inheritance or otherwise).

Wow. I sound really cynical. I'm not, you know. I'm just very sad and very scared. My mom is all I've got.

And, well, you can see it pretty clearly. My mom is getting older, and she has not taken care of herself. She has a tough time getting around because of her hips and sometimes her knees, and she's definitely overweight.

I would not call her morbidly obese, but she is at least 50 pounds overweight. I guess that's "plump" in today's world. She may get a pass from society, but nature won't give it to her. I think she's fated to suffer more rather than less if she doesn't make a few changes -- now.

But she won't.

The other day I watched a classic movie in which a guy tried to kill his wealthy wife. He sawed off the steps to the basement, then lured her there by creating some sort of emergency there. As luck would have it, she did not step on the booby-trapped wooden steps. Instead, his secret paramour stepped on the steps, flew off them, and snapped her neck.

I laughed.

Then I pulled up a recording of the American Ballet Theatre's production of Frederick Ashton's "The Dream." It's a one-act ballet based on *A Midsummer Night's Dream* -- enchanted woods, music by Mendelssohn ...

It was glorious. My head is still full of the images and the music.

CHAPTER NINE

Welcome to Cat Dump Bridge.

Okay, that's not the real name of the bridge. The real name is Moon Bridge, and was modeled after ones you might see in China or Japan, or San Francisco's Golden Gate Park, for that matter. The original idea, I think, was to make it good for cars and people. But, well, if you've seen a moon bridge, you know that they're really steep -- when you go up the moon, you climb a ladder, and when you descend, you do the same.

Moon Bridges are beautiful. They present a gorgeous arc over a stream, and usually they're flanked by lovely trees and flowering bushes.

The bridge is steep and it has high walls. It's perfect for hunkering down with your bag cats or kittens before you hurl them over the edge and into the streambed below. You wait, wait, wait for the splash -- the "dust to dust" moment. But -- you don't hear it because there's no water in the stream bed. It's just a river of rocks and sand, trashed out with paper bags and plastic bottles. Sometimes you see work gangs from the local jail in a "fresh air outing" in their orange jumpsuits, picking up the trash.

Hey, but this is an upscale neighborhood and we don't have trash and we don't tolerate animal abuse.

Yeah, sure.

Moon Bridge was built at the same time they built the park. It was in the 1930s, and the idea of incorporating Japanese or Chinese lanterns, lights, pathways, and rock gardens was really popular.

What would you do if someone bundled up all your hopes and dreams, crammed them into a dirty paper bag, then hurled them over a crumbling Moon Bridge, where the ladder was missing rungs on not just the "up" side, but also the "down"? What would you do if someone laughed in your face at your willingness to go all poetic and say the bag of cats was equivalent to your hopes and dreams thrown over the ledge, to go crashing onto the dirt, rocks, and trash?

Would you understand that they were laughing because they were angry? Would you accept their outrage -- that you had the audacity to conflate your trivial histrionics with the flesh and blood lives of sentient beings?

Well, I don't know what to say except to say that I think that my stupid emotions mean nothing. I'm ridiculous. My thoughts are ridiculous. My feelings are ridiculous.

The cats that are hurled from the bridge matter a lot more than my feelings, which are nothing more than projections of my mental state and are, by definition, solipsistic, even narcissistic. When we look at the cats - the kittens, actually -- we're talking about flesh and blood. We're talking about beings that will cease to exist the minute their little heads crack against the rocks, or when they die slowly, painfully, of dehydration (which is how, by the way, I saw my grandmother die).

Someone should shove me into a big paper bag and hurl me off a super-high Moon Bridge and then laugh when I hit the cobbles, dirt, and cracking Diet Coke bottles.

Go ahead, hate me.

After all, I hate myself.

CHAPTER TEN

He's been messing with her checks.

I don't know why my mother doesn't see it. Further, I don't know what she sees in him. I guess she's falling for his flattery, which surprises me. She's usually not a pushover. In fact, if anything, she's a hardcore cynic. But, you know how it is, the people with the toughest shells usually have the softest interiors. Just consider the oyster (or the clam). Okay, you're probably asking, "Where's the pearl?" That pearl is me (haha). Yes, I'm the infinitely valuable and beautiful result of years of constant irritation. Yep, that's me.

Well, I'm going to do what I can to see what Mr. Sneaky is doing to my mom. First of all, I'm going to check into his background. I don't believe anything about him. Let's start with his name. He introduced himself as Chase Branch. Come on! Who can possibly believe that??? Why not just call yourself "ATM" or "Citicard" -- it's ridiculous.

If, perchance, he does have that sad misfortune of possessing a name that makes him sound like one of the "too big to fail" banks, well, I'll have to accept it. At the same time, I think it's just a bit too conveniently evocative of a stage name; perhaps of a hypnotist or other type illusionist.

I can tell you right now, I'm not buying it. He's up to no good, and I think I've caught him in at least one of his imbroglios.

Last night, as I was coming up the secret passageway from the basement where I'm building my Cat Rescue Care Center (grandiose dreams, modest actualization, but hey, you do what you can, right?), I was trying my best to not make the wooden stairs creak, so I paused next to the door that goes into the utility room next to the kitchen. The secret passageway gives me the option to come out through the utility room or in the end of the entryway hallway. I usually take the entryway hallway secret door because it's very close to the stairway and I can run up to my room without worrying too much about discovery.

Not that my mom would ever know or remember ... by that time at night, she's "asleep" on the couch, where she has a couple fuzzy soft throw blankets that came in the mail as a gift from one of the numerous Native American education projects she donates to. Okay, so she's not cynical about everything -- in fact, in the case of this constellation of tribal outreach / child education programs, I think she's something of an easy mark. I wonder if she even realizes she's donating to twelve or so, rather than one. Their marketing materials are virtually indistinguishable, which is perhaps a good thing, since it means she gets 12 gifts of appreciation rather than just one.

So, Mom has a lot of fleecy throws, each with tribal designs.

To get back to the moment of revelation -- it was around 7 pm, and he should have been gone by that time, by for some reason, he was still in the house. Usually, he left around 6 with some sort of excuse that he had to go somewhere for a dinner meeting. I was always very glad to see him leave.

He was in the utility room and he had the box that Mom uses for her checkbooks and also receipts. He was quickly going through the checks and some of the bank statements. I saw him pull a single check from a checkbook and put it in his pocket, then he stopped, grabbed an entire checkbook and put it in his jacket pocket.

I thought of bursting into the room and attacking him, but I'm small, and he's obviously experienced and cagey. I would never win. Not only would he physically harm me, he'd twist everything around and my mom would not know what to believe. She would probably continue to believe him -- after all what fat woman who gets absolutely no male attention is capable of willingly throwing away the only source of affirmation she has? Also, he came with the added bonus of not questioning her drinking or pills.

Mr. Chase Branch. You're history. I'm going to figure this out, and you're not going to like it.

But, I'm going to be smart about it. I've learned from you. I'll play my cards close to my chest, and things will work out.

I exited the secret passageway through the entrance hallway secret door, and crept up quietly to my room. Once in my room, I made a point of doing a bit of Polish clogging I learned in a folk dancing class I took last year. It was nice and noisy. After about ten minutes, I figured that Mr. Chase Branch would have completed his thievery, and would be back whispering sycophantic nothings in Mom's unhearing ear.

It was time for my grand entrance.

I clattered down the stairs and zoomed from room to room -- "I can fly! I can fly!" doing my favorite Peter Pan imitation, turning myself into a leaping embodiment of the refusal to grow up as I prepared to meet Mr. Overgrown Lost Boy.

"Ho Ho -- hale and hearty, me smartie!" I shouted as I leapt into the room where Mr. Chase Branch lounged in the smooth brown leather reclining chair my mom had positioned in front of the television.

"Well, Lulu, very nice to see you!" said Mr. Chase Branch.

My mother rubbed her eyes as she roused herself from her semi-stuporous state.

"Chase, you're still here?" she asked. I knew she was deeply ashamed of having her inebriate state witnessed like this. It was good. She would compel him to leave.

Chase looked at her, then at me.

"I was just leaving, sweetheart," he said. "You look beautiful."

In point of fact, she did not. Her eyes were swollen, her face mashed in on side, and her hair tousled and frowzy. She looked more bloated than usual, and there was an embarrassing, flesh-revealing gap between her long-sleeve t-shirt and her gray sweatpants.

"Isn't it your bedtime?" he asked me.

"Always," I said. I wasn't getting drawn in so easily.

"It has been nice to be here," said Chase. He gathered his things, and then looked to his jacket which he had draped over a chair.

"I can get your jacket," I said. I was curious to see how he would react.

"That's okay. I've got it." Chase moved quickly when motivated.

He left.

Now I had to think of what to do about his malfeasance with my mother's checks.

CHAPTER ELEVEN

It is very strange to live in these times, and to be a kid. At least that's what I've concluded after surveying my own situation and that of the people I know from school, from dance, and from the various places I visit and have contact with.

I'm not really talking about politics or economic times or religion or technology or any of the things people usually talk about when they want to express dismay at how we live and the annoyingly rapid rate of change.

No, I'm talking about fathers and daughters; fathers and sons. Why is it that almost every single kid I know has an absent or partially absent father?

Take my neighbors, Kithie and Gus Wexthrall. Kithie won't really talk about her dad. Apparently he's not dead, but his engagement with her is minimal. He might as well be dead. He sends her postcards and money. That's it. I only know this because I happened to overhear her mom talking on her cell phone while I was poking around their fence looking for leaf specimens for my science class.

Gus's dad was kidnapped by a weird stalker who had a crush on Kithie's mom, who was, back in the day, when she was a child star of Family Plot, a comedy series that featured a family of vampires. Kithie's mom was the cute little girl vampire, Little Anna, and she had a really strong fan base. She still receives checks for residuals and is invited to nostalgia events. I guess the stalker just got caught up in the celebrity & nostalgia stuff and lost control. It was all over the news, mainly because the stalker / kidnapper turned out to be the school principal. He was so desperate to get close to Kithie's mom that he dressed up in women's clothing and pretended to be Gus's dad's sister. It would be funny if it weren't so pathetic.

When the principal was arrested and Gus's dad came back, the principal was finally able to get the psychological help he needed.

So, because Gus's dad was forced to leave, and did not do so on his own volition, he won the "best dad" award in my book.

I guess the kids whose dads are in the military and are deployed, or who work out of town should not be punished or marked down. They probably keep in touch as they can: text messages, phone calls, emails, posts to social network sites. I just don't think it's the same as having a dad who's there to give you a pat on the back when you need it, or a stern talking-to when you think you don't need his guidance.

In most cases, the kids don't have a dad because the dad decided to leave. Sometimes there's a divorce. Sometimes there's not -- they just took off. Many never actually married the mom, which makes keeping touch much harder, especially if they took off when the kid was small.

Sometimes the mom fled the dad. Sometimes the mom disappeared, and then the dad disappeared, too. Those kids have a particularly rough time of it -- they live with grandparents, relatives, foster families, or, in some cases, they become part of the invisible homeless who are scrambling on their own -- sometimes with an older sister or brother trying to fill the gap.

You'd think this "fatherless family" phenomenon would be taking place in poor neighborhoods, but it's not. It's darn near ubiquitous. The only reason why there hasn't been a public outcry is, in my opinion, because many families are "blended."

Fake fathers.

Who's the "dad du jour"?

Is the new dad really an adequate surrogate? I argue "no" because these surrogates tend to come and go. The average kid I know has had at least three "dad" figures in his or her life by the time they're 13 or 14. The worst is that no one listens. They're supposed to welcome each "dad du jour" with welcome arms, as though each one were the real dad, but the real one's usually gone totally prodigal, and when he does bother to come back, it's awkward and sad because of all the emotions that have to be tamped down and kept under the surface. Heaven help you if you want to talk about the way that life has been in the rollercoaster of aroused and then dashed hopes, dreams, and expectations.

I'm trying not to hate my own dad.

It's easiest to forgive my dad if I focus my anger on my mom. Yes, I blame Mom.

In reality, I blame myself.

CHAPTER TWELVE

I didn't pay any attention to the blank-faced guy walking down the street clutching a brown paper bag in his left hand until a tall, blonde guy wearing a hoodie emerged from the liquor store in the strip mall.

"Hey! HEY!" he shouted. The guy I decided was the owner of the liquor store started running.

The owner of the liquor store pulled out an enormous handgun -- some kind of hand-cannon, in my opinion -- and totally unnecessary for the job at hand.

The guy carrying the brown paper bag turned, apparently trying to decide whether to run or, well, perhaps shoot. Who knows what he had in his brown paper bag or on his person. It is, after all, a "conceal and carry" state. He had a remarkably blank look on his face, almost as though he were carrying out someone or something's bidding. It was hard to tell.

It was going to be a gunfight in the parking lot, I didn't want to catch a stray bullet, so I looked around at where I could hide, or some car to dive under.

It didn't come to that. He saw the gun, and if he had one, it must have been a petite shadow or simulacrum of this one, and so he chose to give up his pilfered wares, in this case a large bottle of clear bright blue liquid. Yuk. Probably 100 proof, with sugar. It was the sort of thing that Mom would most likely drink if she wanted to imagine herself on a Caribbean cruise.

"Uh man, sorry. I forgot about paying for this." His whole being screamed deception and insincerity. There was something very strange about his aura. It was as though his energy pulled back inside him, and his eyes seemed to retreat.

"Hand it over. You don't have to give me the one you legitimately paid for," he said.

The guy handed over the bottle. The label said BLUE HOOCH.

The liquor store owner noticed me standing rigid and still in the parking lot. The shoplifter walked quickly down the street and disappeared into a side street.

"Sorry about that. The little punk came in, bought a bottle of vodka, then went into the back room and stuck this bottle into his brown bag. It seriously pissed me off."

"I was trying to think of where to hide to not get caught in the crossfire, but there's no place to go out here," I said.

"The little punk gave it up once he saw this," said the liquor store owner, proud of his hand-cannon.

"How much did that bottle cost?" I asked. He was looking at it. He was still breathing hard.

"About 18 bucks or so."

"Oh." I had a hard time believing that any court of law would think that shoplifting a bottle of "Blue Hooch" justified lethal force.

But, people will do anything to "win."

Some people are open and take a front-on approach, and will threaten you with a huge gun or dog if you do something they perceive as harmful to them.

Others are sneaky. They'll find a way to do something nasty and potentially really damaging. They'll sabotage you. They'll stick knives in so quickly you don't even know where and when it has happened.

I wondered if the shoplifter guy would feel so humiliated that he'd be back to do something sneaky and horrible. I wonder if the liquor store owner did the right thing. Sure, he did defend his territory and he communicated the message that you can't mess with him. I don't know. Lots of ways to look at this.

Some people take the idea of winning to their own psyche. Some turn the other cheek, which is to say they have mastered the art of ignoring things that do not really matter in the overall scheme of things.

Others internalize the trauma and then brutalize themselves as they reenact the initial event in an attempt to come to terms with it all.

Getting even. What a stupid concept. But, sometimes you have to take a stand to stop bad things from happening. Sometimes you don't have a lot of pull in the world and you just have to do what you can do.

CHAPTER THIRTEEN

The part of town where Lulu lived used to be considered the most upscale and prestigious in the city. Oh, but how times change.

The mortgage and housing booms and busts were tsunamis that churned through the collective consciousness, first as grandiose "build myself a castle and flip it for a huge profit" dreams that led to over-leveraging their revenue streams and their future. Booms were characterized by easy credit, housing development spawnings and "soi-disant" real estate mogul wannabes. Boom-boom build. These waves crushed everything in their path like bulldozer phoenixes that rose up shiny, trendy, and above all, flashy.

The busts were equally potent tsunamis triggered by a sharp jolt of vicious seismicity in the credit and capital markets. Stock market crash? Credit drying up? Economic collapse in Asia? Fiscal crisis in Europe? The waves churned and obliterated entire neighborhoods as people defaulted on their loans, foreclosures were rampant, and the homes that were not abandoned were neglected for years. Newly displaced people and pets started living largely underground lives. There were attempts to squat in abandoned outbuildings, but they were thwarted by gangs of neighborhood vigilantes.

Blight.

There is something tragic about a "shabbed-out" neighborhood. It's shabby, but the shabbiness does not feel natural. It's not like one of the neighborhoods that got shabby because the owners aged and became unable to take care of their houses. That's a shabbiness born of benign neglect, and although it's sad to contemplate the relative isolation of the older residents, at least they're living in their homes and have not yet been medicated into a state of drooling complacence as they stare at the television or at nothing at all. The "benign neglect" homes tend to have little gardens (smaller each year as the owners' mobility declines) and fading paint (as the owners' eyesight declines).

"Shabbed out" usually is an indication of absentee ownership. Rentals.

Bare bones maintenance.

Meridian lives in one of those homes.

The neighborhood is between where I live and my school. It's behind Neko Sushi (which has not yet changed its name! Note to self: visit them again. Up the ante.)

Her parents were employed in manufacturing, but when the plants shut down, they found themselves out of work. Going back to school was not an option -- not enough money, not enough time. To their credit, neither the mom nor the dad was addicted to anything.

But, the options were not good. They ended up in the food service industry. It was hard to go from $38 per hour with benefits to $8.28 and no benefits, except one free meal per shift. Meridian's dad thought about getting into welding. There were many jobs, but it would take a year, and the cost would be around $35,000. He would not be able to work, so would have to take out loans, which would put the indebtedness at around $70,000. At the end of the day, he'd have to travel to wherever the work was, which would eat up much of the additional wage. So, was it worth it? So far, they could not decide.

So, both mom and dad worked two jobs. Meridian raised herself. At least that's what it looked like to me.

I met Meridian one afternoon on one of those crazy days I thought it would be a great idea to combine my dance with skateboarding. There's an old park near her home, with an old wading pool that no longer has any water in it. It's perfectly dry and it makes a perfect place to practice ollies and all the other moves I'm not usually able to practice because I run into a curb, a joint, or a rough spot in the sidewalk or driveway.

Meridian is small and compact, with dark skin and hair that she wears in dozens of tiny braids adorned with colorful beads that click softly when she moves her head. Her eyes are warm brown, intelligent and curious, and she has this way of listening that makes you feel like whatever you're saying is the most important thing in the world.

I knocked on Meridian's front door. Her mother answered, looking very tense. She was buttoning the cloth jacket with her name monogrammed on the pocket, and it appeared she was late to work. It wasn't clear where she worked, but it appeared perhaps it was a uniform for work in a casino.

"Is Meridian home? Can she play?"

"You're a very polite little girl. Very few people actually ask permission. They just text and then expect their friend to show up."

I clasped my hands in front of me and squeezed them tightly together. I squeezed my eyes at the same time. I did not want Meridian's mom to see the tears that suddenly appeared there.

Meridian ran up behind her mom.

"I'm not allowed to play outside when my mom and dad are at work. I have to stay inside. Lock the doors."

The mental image of a little girl my own age barricaded in her home every afternoon rather than being able to go outside and roam around suddenly filled me with a cold chill. I was glad for the change of emotional surge. What a relief. My tears dried up.

Solitary confinement can't be good for nine-year-old girls, even if the goal is safety.

Meridian's mom looked at me, then down at her smartphone to check the time.

"Lulu, I trust you. You can play until 5:00 pm, but then you'll need to go back home. I don't want you to be walking alone after dark."

"It's okay. My mom doesn't mind." I did not bother to say that my mom not only did not mind, she did not know. I always tried to be back by 6, though, just in case she had gotten herself into any kind of trouble.

"I'm sure she does. But, even if she doesn't, I don't want to run any risks. You and Meridian can play together. Perhaps you can work on homework together. Meridian would like that. Be sure to lock the doors and do not let anyone in under any circumstances."

"I don't mind being alone," Meridian tells me the first time I visit. "I've got books and homework and my art supplies. But sometimes I wish I had someone to talk to, you know?"

I do know. Loneliness is like a physical ache, something you carry in your chest until you forget it's not supposed to be there.

Meridian draws constantly -- detailed pencil sketches of buildings and trees and people, but also fantastical creatures that exist only in her imagination. Dragons with butterfly wings, cats with stars for eyes, foxes that can fly. When I tell her about my rescue operation in the basement, she doesn't think I'm crazy. Instead, she asks if she can help.

"My parents won't be home until midnight," she says. "I could come over after school, help you feed them and clean their spaces. I'm good with animals."

It's the first time in months that I don't feel completely alone.

CHAPTER FOURTEEN

Behind our neighborhood, past the failing strip mall and the empty lots where houses used to stand, runs Willow Creek. It's not much of a creek anymore -- more like a muddy stream that floods when it rains and dries to a trickle in summer. But the trees along its banks create a green corridor through the city, a place where wild things can still exist.

This is where I find most of the animals I rescue. This is where people dump the pets they don't want anymore, thinking they'll "live free" or "find their way." What they really find is hunger, predators, and cars.

The creek is also where the homeless camp has sprung up -- a collection of tents and tarps and makeshift shelters hidden among the trees. The people there know about the abandoned animals, and sometimes they'll call to me when I'm walking the path.

"Hey, little girl," an old woman named Dorothy calls out one afternoon. "There's a dog down by the water. Been there two days. Won't let nobody near him, but he's hurt bad."

Dorothy is maybe sixty, with gray hair tied back in a bandana and clothes that have seen better decades. Her hands are rough and calloused, but her eyes are kind. She lives in a blue tarp tent with her partner Miguel, and they've been feeding stray cats with their own food stamps.

I find the dog where she said I would -- a medium-sized mutt with matted brown fur and a gash on his side that's going septic. He growls when he sees me, all bared teeth and fear, but I can see the pain in his eyes.

"It's okay," I whisper, pulling a can of dog food from my backpack. "I'm not going to hurt you."

It takes three days of patient visits before he'll let me close enough to help. I name him Braveheart, because even hurt and abandoned, he never stops fighting.

The wild creatures are different from the abandoned pets. There's a family of raccoons that live in the storm drains, and they've learned that I bring food. The mama raccoon is missing her left front paw -- probably caught in a trap somewhere -- but she's fierce and protective of her three babies. I call her Bandit, and she watches me with intelligent dark eyes as I leave dishes of cat food near the drain entrance.

There's also a red fox with an injured leg that I found limping through the park. The veterinarian books I borrowed from the library helped me understand that wild animals need different care than domestic ones. This fox -- I call him Rusty because his fur is the color of autumn leaves -- is my greatest challenge. He's wild but not wild enough to survive on his own, too proud to accept help but too hurt to refuse it.

"You don't have to like me," I whisper to him as I change his bandages in the basement. "You just have to let me help you."

His dark eyes seem to understand everything, and sometimes I think he knows more about the world than I do.

CHAPTER FIFTEEN

You are beautiful, cool, and kind.

You are beautiful, smart, and strong.

I like you -- you are GREAT! I like you -- you are GREAT!

I am experimenting with running those thoughts through my head whenever I'm in a public place.

Why?

It's all about brain waves. I was watching The Discovery Channel and there was a program about how engineers have found they can measure brain wave activity outside the head. At first I didn't think anything of it. After all, we're used to seeing men and women measuring with little electrodes adhered to their heads as they toddle off to the sleep lab to see just how and when REM kicks in.

I never thought anything of it.

But, then, someone figured out that if you can measure brain wave activity, you can quantify and characterize it. You can even measure it and then teach people to channel and even intensify certain brain wave patterns. Those brain wave patterns are then connected to a device that uses them to activate digital controls.

So -- people with advanced ALS (Lou Gehrig's disease) can use their brain waves to direct assistive technologies to do things for them ... write, speak, move their wheelchairs.

Again, I didn't think of it, until, in a flash, I realized that our thoughts are perceivable in the phenomenal world, and that our thoughts give out energy -- energy that is not diffuse or vague, but is very, very focused and precise. It's so much so that the engineers have been very successful at creating thought-controlled devices.

Wow.

So, I just wonder how human beings can detect. I'll bet it's more than we suspect.

The implications are pretty staggering. It means that if you have aggressive, hostile thoughts toward someone, chances are, they will pick up on the brain wave activity. Of course, you're probably amplifying the message with scowling and other non-verbal communication, but in a way, that's beside the point.

The real point is that your thoughts leak out. The brain waves are detectable outside the body.

It seems to me that if we really accept that reality, the real challenge to us as human beings is to learn how to discipline ourselves, marshal our thoughts, and proactively enter any space where others will be in physical proximity to you with a small litany of positive, joyous, encouraging, and all-embracing / all-accepting mantras.

If you don't -- if you let yourself be sour and surly, cynical and suspicious -- your brainwaves will trigger defensiveness in the other person.

So -- even if the person you are encountering seeks to get the best of you, you can't let yourself sink to their level. You have to take the high road and chant to yourself thoughts that are positive, affirming, and all-embracing.

Do I really think this will work?

Well, to tell the truth, yes. I do.

What exactly would happen if all I transmit are positive, affirming, "I think you're the absolute BEST' thoughts?

I have no idea. But, starting tomorrow at 5 am in the morning, I'm officially combining my philosophy of living, which is to not indulge in open, cynical, sneering, or mocking attitudes, with big, big thoughts and positive affirmations...

I am just so, so, curious to see what kind of results I'll have (if any)...

You are beautiful, cool, and kind.

You are beautiful, smart, and strong.

You are beautiful, cool, and kind.

You are beautiful, smart, and strong

You are beautiful, cool, and kind.

You are beautiful, smart, and strong

Are you feeling it??

CHAPTER SIXTEEN

Computer chips are made of silicon. Silicon is ideal for storing digital data. It can record frequencies and vibrations of all kinds.

How about silicon dioxide crystals (also known as quartz crystals)?

Could quartz crystals be nature's silicon chips, and they've been recording data for eons, and they could play everything back if only we knew how to retrieve and "play" them?

How do you tap into the quartz crystals? What's the code?

And, what kind of "codes" and "vibrations" have they been recording? Are the so-called "hums" and even sitings of images and weird vibrations actually releases of data from the quartz crystals?

The thin, serious-faced young girl was not looking as pulled-together as she usually did when she stood on the sidewalk in front of Neko Sushi with the two or three cats she usually brought with her. A calico and a Siamese sat in the cat-carrier at her feet, and a small black and white tabby purred as she cradled him in her arms.

"Don't worry, Sebastian. We're going to let the world know that cats are not really used for sushi and it's not funny to confuse people," she whispered.

It was her goal to be on the Neko Sushi sidewalk for at least 30 minutes each day after she finished her homework and before dance practice.

"Lucky Cat Sushi" or "Lucky Neko Sushi" NOT "Neko Sushi" -- CHANGE THE NAME NOW!

Her hand-lettered sign had proved surprisingly durable. Passers-by glanced at her curiously. Employees walked by and smiled as they acknowledged her.

The few people who got it, though, were never to be seen.

The people who had the power and authority to reconfigure perception by naming / renaming, and to push identity into flux so that it could be reformed, reshaped, and revisited, were never around.

"Are you trying to adopt your cats?" asked one woman.

"They've already been rescued once. Why would I put them through the same thing twice?" replied the thin, serious-faced young girl.

The woman, whose face seemed stretched across her cheekbones, and whose hair was a shade of red found only in the false color composites once in satellite imagery of the earth, looked closely at Lulu. She was not sure whether or not to take what she had said as an insult.

Finally, given Lulu's age -- probably 8, perhaps 9 at best -- she gave her the benefit of the doubt.

"Be nice to your kitties," said the woman.

"Always," intoned Lulu.

After her daily ritual of "Occupy Neko Sushi," Lulu liked to go into the shop next door.

Gem Magic.

It wasn't really a store that sold gemstones. What it really sold were crystals that were or had been popular with the New Age crowd.

Lulu loved the quartz crystals.

"These are from Hot Springs, Arkansas," said the owner.

"I'm glad you like the geodes. The crystals are quartz," explained the owner.

"But they're purple," said Lulu.

"True. That makes them amethyst. It's a variety of quartz. Same chemical composition, though. Silicon dioxide."

"Oh."

That was it.

CHAPTER SEVENTEEN

Despite being Kithie's little brother, Gus is nothing like her. Where she's all sharp edges and storm clouds, he's sunshine and scattered energy. His red curls bounce when he walks, and his green eyes light up when he talks about code like other kids talk about sports or movies.

He's also the only person in our neighborhood who knows about my computer skills, though he doesn't know the extent of them. We met online in a coding forum where I use the handle "SilentMouse" and he goes by "RedFox01." We'd been chatting for months before we realized we were neighbors.

"You're the ballet girl," he said the first time we met in person, behind the 7-Eleven where we'd agreed to finally meet face-to-face.

"You're the kid who hacked the school's attendance system," I replied.

We grinned at each other, two misfits recognizing kindred spirits.

Gus is lonely too, though he hides it better than I do. His sister's reputation follows him everywhere, and kids at school either avoid him or want to pump him for information about Kithie. His mom is always performing, always "on," and there's no room in that performance for a son who just wants to build robots and write code.

"Want to see something cool?" he asks me one day, pulling out a small device that looks like a cross between a phone and a calculator.

"What is it?"

"Motion detector I built from scratch. I'm going to hide them around the neighborhood, create a network that tracks movement patterns. Like, did you know that at 3:17 every morning, someone walks through the park carrying something heavy?"

I did know that, actually. That someone is me, carrying bags of food to the animals by the creek. But I don't tell Gus this. Instead, I ask if he can help me with a different kind of problem.

"I need to access some financial records," I say. "Legally," I add quickly. "They belong to my family."

Gus raises an eyebrow. "Someone trying to scam your mom?"

"Something like that."

"I'm in."

CHAPTER EIGHTEEN

"Hello, little Lulu. It's very nice to see you again," he said. He was back. Now he was wearing tasseled loafers.

The doorbell had rung and I ran as fast as I could to answer it. I wanted to see if there was indication that he knew he had been busted and that his little scheme to forge my mother's checks was not going to work.

My mother turned the corner and approached down the long hallway. She was wobbling a bit, but not as much as usual. Sometimes it was hard to tell if she wobbled due to inebriation or from her bad hips and knees. Being overweight and giving up on exercise had taken a toll on her.

"Well, Sugar Plum, you look very sweet today," he said. He wasn't talking to me. He was talking to my mom. I was invisible to him most of the time, which is just how I wanted it.

"You call my mom 'Sugar Plum'?" I asked. I was incredulous. It was not really very nice. It was infantilizing and mocking. At least that was how I saw it. However, Mom seemed to like it, but I think she was just going along with it because she wanted to catch the wave of affirmation and male attention.

"I like that color on you," he said. Mom looked down at her dark purple velour hoodie and the matching yoga pants (although it was laughable to think of Mom in any yoga poses), and her sparkly sandals. She was wearing a paisley headband and large chandelier earrings. It was, everything considered, a relatively flattering ensemble, which is not easy to do if you're pushing 200 pounds.

Clearly she had been expecting him.

"I've got our shows and I'll make us some snacks," she said. Somehow Mom had convinced him that the new forensics and crime drama series were great "date night" viewing. Maybe they were. For my money, if I couldn't watch Baryshnikov, I'd like to watch Animal Planet or Discovery channel programming. They were more authentic and told you something about the human condition. My favorite was "Fatal Attractions" which followed the predictably grisly outcome of befriending wild animals, to the point that people considered them their children.

Perhaps the most horrifying episode in "Fatal Attractions" involved a young adult male chimp who tore the face off his owner when she came back to the car with a new hair color and "do."

The animal behaviorist explained it away saying the chimp did not realize she was the same person, so when she got into the driver's seat, he was nervous and thought he needed to kill the intruder.

My response? Bogus! Chimps can smell, can't they? They're animals, after all. They know who people are -- a hairstyle changes nothing.

My opinion? I think the chimp was just a dominating, controlling animal who decided to punish his significant other for not checking with him before changing her appearance: You didn't ask my permission first? Well, I'll fix that! I'm ripping your face off. (!)

I'm not sure he knew he would be successful at inflicting so much damage. The chimp seemed rather somber before the police and animal control officers shot him to death.

I don't want to go so far to say it mirror patriarchy, and it's exactly what happens in the human realm, because I'm not so dogmatically feminist.

Come to think of it, I do wish my mom and her "guy" would watch Fatal Attractions. Maybe I can put it in the mix -- mislabel an episode and perhaps they would watch it through. My mom could see the consequences of dating an animal.

They'll tear your face off. They'll bite you and you'll hemorrhage to death before help can come. They'll go alpha on you and sink their teeth into your throat.

"Mom. Do you want me to run down to the Corner Market to get croissants, brie, raspberry confit?" I asked.

"That would be very sweet. Yes, I'd love you to do that. Go grab my purse -- you can take my wallet."

It was great that my mom trusted me. She should. I always have her back. I will do whatever I can to protect her.

As I walked down to the Corner Market, I pulled out her cell phone and called the credit card companies and declared her cards lost / stolen. I wasn't taking any chances. Once he found out that the bank had already been alerted to fraudulent activity / identity theft on her account, he might try to start taking whatever he could get his hands on.

I don't know why these guys who try to work my mom think they can get away with things. I guess it's because they can and they have.

Don't get me wrong. My mom is smart. But, she has some serious "issues."

Again, I need to protect her.

You might say I'm enabling her. I probably am. But, what can I do? I'm nine years old. I can't really force her into rehab, and if I did, what would happen to me? Where would I go? The only relative I have is my dad, and he's somewhere in Colombia, as far as I know, and my mom certainly isn't telling.

The night everything comes to a head, Mom is more drunk than usual, and Chase Branch is getting bold. I hear them arguing in the living room -- him pushing her to sign some papers, her slurring that she needs to "think about it" first.

From my hiding spot in the secret passageway, I can see him getting frustrated. His smooth mask is slipping, revealing something ugly underneath.

"Listen, Sugar Plum," he says, and his voice has an edge now. "I've been very patient with you. Very understanding. But this opportunity won't last forever."

"What opportunity?" Mom asks, squinting at the papers in her hand.

"The investment opportunity I told you about. But I need you to sign tonight, or we'll lose it."

I know what those papers really are -- I used Gus's equipment to photograph them last week. They're not investment forms. They're loan applications using our house as collateral, applications that would put us hundreds of thousands of dollars in debt while putting the money directly into Chase's account.

I can't let this happen. I can't let him steal our home.

Taking a deep breath, I step out of the passageway and into the living room.

"Mom, don't sign those."

Chase whirls around, his face flushed with anger and surprise. "Lulu! What are you doing up? It's past your bedtime."

"Those aren't investment papers," I say, ignoring him and speaking directly to Mom. "They're loan applications. He's trying to steal our house."

"Don't be ridiculous," Chase says, but his voice is too loud, too defensive. "Your daughter has quite an imagination."

I pull out my phone and show Mom the photos I've taken -- Chase going through her financial papers, copying her credit card information, the real forms behind the fake investment documents.

"I've been documenting everything," I say. "I have recordings too."

Mom stares at the phone screen, and for the first time in months, her eyes look sharp and focused.

"Get out," she says quietly.

"Now wait a minute, Sugar Plum--"

"GET OUT!" Mom roars, and suddenly she's not the broken woman on the couch anymore. She's the business consultant who used to turn failing companies around, the woman who doesn't take crap from anyone.

Chase tries to argue, tries to convince her that I'm lying, but Mom is fully awake now. She's seen the evidence. She knows the truth.

After he leaves -- slamming the door and shouting threats about "ungrateful bitches" -- Mom and I sit together in the suddenly quiet living room.

"How long have you known?" she asks.

"Since the beginning."

"Why didn't you tell me sooner?"

"Would you have believed me?"

She's quiet for a long time, staring at her hands. "Probably not."

"Mom," I say carefully, "we need to talk. About the drinking. About the pills. About Dad."

She starts crying then -- big, ugly sobs that shake her whole body. I climb onto the couch beside her and let her hold me while she cries out months of pain and shame and regret.

"I'm so sorry, baby," she whispers. "I'm so, so sorry."

CHAPTER NINETEEN

Have you ever wanted something so much that it hurts?

Did you know that what you wanted was not ever going to be there for you?

How did you feel when you had that moment of realization?

How did you deal with it?

What did you do?

I want to know because I need to understand how and where and how to deal with irreparable ruptures, longings I just can't deal with, and the meanings of life that I just don't understand ... and moreover, I don't want to understand.

Where are we? Where can we go from here?

How are we going to answer that question?

The day was fine. It was chilly but I was okay with it. I walked around, I made my usual stops. Things were the same, nothing new, nothing extraordinary. But I felt extraordinarily sad, extraordinarily in need of connection. Where are you? When can I see you? What will you say to me when and where we connect? Can't you tell me?

Crisp air, blue sky, sweat on my belly and on the small of my back as I run, run, run back home.

Then, I pull together the things I need for dance class. I'll get there two hours early, but this is Saturday and no one will mind. I'll be there, and I'll put on my headphones and I'll do whatever I need to do to deal with this moment, with this longing, with the way I feel just lost, abandoned, thrown out to the farthest star in the galaxy and how that makes me feel sad, sad, sad, and yes -- with surging feelings I don't want to define but they feel a lot like ... say it! ... rage...

Okay, Mom. Mom, Mom, Mom.... Why can't you pull yourself together??
Why do I have to be the mom and you the child? Why can't you get yourself
off the leather couch and take note of what I am and how I am who I am...
love, love, love... oh yes it's just so hard ...love, love, love... it's something I
no longer want to feel -- ever, ever, ever...

Mother, oh Mother. Get yourself up out of your grave and pull yourself
together... you know you can do it and so why don't you? Why do you have to
bury yourself years, years, years before you actually die?

Why do you have to go all "radio silent" on me and just lie there passed out
on the couch where I have to look at you all dead and buried to the sentient
world and I have to pull my heart up out of my belly and tell you Yes! I
forgive you! Yes! I forgive you! I can't hate because hate only hurts me & it
does nothing at all to the world outside and it won't make you do anything but
push yourself deeper into your own spiritual death... oh yes oh yes ..

And here we are, dear Mother... wake up. But oh my, I know I can't continue
to push myself against the pure granite of reality without bruising myself (and
no one else)...

Run, run, run, rabbit, run ... dance dance dance sparrow dance....

I'm flying up to the sun and you can't tell me what I need to hear. Oh no. I'm
too far gone. Oh yes, I'm too far out of my mind ... dance, dance.

I put on my leotard. It is black. I dance in a classical studio, you see. I put on
my tights. They are pink. I dance in a classical studio you see. I put on my
slippers. They are leather, and when I received them, I had to sew on the
elastic band that kept my feet inside. I suppose it's a tradition dating back to
the French, and hey I'm totally fine with that. I would much rather not live in
this era ...I'd much rather be back in 19th century France. And, oh yes, let me
tell you what it's all about when I talk to my favorite writers .. Balzac,
Stendhal, Flaubert, and well you know already -- Zola.

I ride my bicycle as fast as I possibly can ...

I arrive. I push my bicycle into the anteroom where they'll let me keep it. I run into the small classroom that's never used at this time of the day. It's Saturday, after all. Most classes are after school during the week. I stretch, I stretch, I stretch... and I do not, do not, do not..... think... remember... reflect.

No!

I stretch, I stretch, I stretch ... and then I ready myself to dance. Does anyone know or see? I hope so. I hope not. I strap my iPod to my arm. I position my earbuds. I have put my favorite songs in a playlist I can repeat over and over and over again.

Oh don't tell me what I already know.

Don't tell me you're worried about me. I'm worried, too, but not about what you might think. You know, or don't you? I worry that one day the magic will just "pop" and not in a good way. It will "pop" and will either push me to the heights so I'm the dancer with the red shoes who dances until her feet leave long stripes of blood on the floor... or will throw me against the wall, and I'll hit it hard and then just crumple to the floor, all broken and half-conscious, needing you, needing your words, needing your warm hand on my forehead...

While I "pop" again... drag myself to my feet, crawl back out there, and then push, push, push myself to dance, stretch, leap, do the most amazing port-a-bras, split leaps, pas-des-chats, rapid-fire tondues -- everything classical and yet not -- so postmodern it hurts ...

Oh yes that is where I am right now ... and utterly unable to say it or articulate the words... so just trust me that perhaps if you let me run, dance, leap, stretch that some day I'll be okay...

....

And still Mother lies stretched out, slow-slow-dying, on the leather sofa in the den, right before my eyes.

CHAPTER TWENTY

Here you are.

Here I am.

What should we do now?

Oh hell. What do I know? I'm not even a teenager yet. All I know is that some days I think I never want to go outside again -- not ever. All I need are two things: first, a way to move my body to music, and second, a way to feed my mind with possibilities of existence that are far, far, far away from anything we have in this ridiculous and hateful mortal coil.

Oh yes.

You know it. I don't have to tell you. You're better at this than I am. All you have to do is put your fingers to the keyboard and already I'm put to shame because you've got it all together. You know how to pull the music, the images, the videos, and the heart-heart-heartbeat of the primordial idea that takes us everywhere and nowhere ... and here I am lost between myth and fairy tale and ugly confession...

And, it just the act of confession that takes me down the rabbit hole.

So don't count on me to confess anything. At least not yet.

I need you too much.

Science. You know it. I know it. We have a love-hate relationship with it. While it seems to promise a kind of immortality of intent -- our thoughts, ideas, shining moments of glory seem so utterly immortal and inextinguishable -- well, it's not like ...

Fall to earth. Yes, dear, Science is the ultimate Icarus.

But before my wax melts and I come crashing to earth, let me talk to you about the latest findings...

Planets outside our solar system. There are dozens and dozens. Many capable of sustaining life.

So why tell me just to let me know that contact is not possible ... and that life on one of those planets just might be sweet and non-predational -- not a word, I know, but something I say to express how terrifically grotesque it seems to me that we live in a world where survival for one means extinction for others, and where it is not possible to balance the population so that everyone gets a fair shake. By "everyone" I mean cave bats, fruit flies, Siberian tigers, companion animals (prisoners to whim, in my opinion), children (companion animals for the lonely adult homo sapiens who are still capable of spawning), tree frogs ... oh I can go on and on.

Why and how and where does science let us do the right thing and get our minds and hearts aligned so we know what do to and how to survive without messing it all up... ??

I love you. I am you. I am determined to be, be, be a Monarch butterfly.

Oh yes, I am just like you, with a circadian clock that helps me sense decreasing day length and which helps me migrate when and where I need to (to the dance studio, to the neighborhood, to Neko Sushi, where I pound, pound for a change of name...)

If I'm just like you, a Monarch butterfly, I have a large number of olfactory receptor genes, which are activated in my antennae and help me interact with other brother and sister monarchs so we can fly together to our ultimate destination...

Unless, of course, those brothers and sisters are just as lost as I am, and we do not actually have brothers and sisters because we are alone -- absolutely alone -- except if we're lucky enough to expand the idea of brotherhood and sisterhood to encompass species way, way, way outside our comfort zone...

But what do I know?

I'm lost, my dear.

I'm just so, so lost.

So I count on you and on the things I find in my scientific journals to put me back in my frequency -- get me vibed in and on track... and to be oriented where I need to be.

Don't forget.

I'm counting on you.

CHAPTER TWENTY-ONE

Recovery isn't linear. It's not like the movies where someone decides to get better and then everything is fine. It's two steps forward, one step back, fighting the same battles over and over until gradually, incrementally, you start winning more than you lose.

Mom goes to rehab -- a 30-day program where she learns to live without wine and pills and self-hatred. While she's gone, I stay with Dorothy and Miguel by the creek, sleeping in a sleeping bag in their tent and helping them care for the animals.

"You're a fierce little warrior," Dorothy tells me one night as we're feeding the cats. "But warriors need to rest sometimes too."

When Mom comes home, she's different. Thinner, clearer, more like the woman in those old photographs. She's still fragile, still taking things one day at a time, but she's present in a way she hasn't been in years.

The first thing she does is help me move my rescue operation upstairs, converting the sunroom into a proper animal sanctuary with veterinary equipment and everything we need to care for injured wildlife.

"I can't believe I never knew about this," she says, watching me change Rusty's bandages. The fox has healed enough to be released back to the wild, but he keeps coming back to visit, like he knows this is a safe place.

"I couldn't tell you. You weren't... available."

"I'm here now," she says. "I'm not going anywhere."

CHAPTER TWENTY-TWO

When something bad or unwelcome happens to me, I like to tell myself that whatever the bad thing is or was, it's all okay. I was probably saved from something hideous. So, I should be grateful -- if not grateful, at least not filled with resentment.

Resentment is bad. It quickly escalates to revenge fantasies. I have to admit that I'm not above revenge fantasies.

For example, when I found out that "Tassel-Toe" was trying to take advantage of my mother and drain her checking account by stealing her identity, besides wanting to see him rot in Hell in the afterlife, I hoped that somehow he would fall in the clutches of a mercenary sex worker (with any luck, Russian -- they're renowned for their ability to strip their prey to the bones, and then turn it over their Mafiosi pimp). He would be stripped of his dignity as she seduced him, then took him for a ride (while she was taking any number of others for a ride).

Oops. I'm nine years old and am not supposed to know about these things, right?

Welcome to the world of raising yourself with the Internet.

Back to my original point: How can you strip someone of their dignity when they've made a practice of not actually having any dignity? It won't work.

Revenge fantasies are futile.

Again, it's better to look at what happened and tell myself I was saved from something hideous.

"Tassel-Toe" will follow his own destiny. I can't really interfere with his karma or whatever good deeds /dharma he decides (however unlikely) to practice.

And, furthermore, this all has to do with my mom, and protecting my mom is not the easiest thing in the world to pull off. I can attest to that, since I've been trying to do so virtually all my life.

It's a different story when it comes to people trying to harm me.

Let me tell you about the kid I like to refer to as "GameBoy Puffiness" -- this is a kid who is constantly playing games on his phone... he's exactly what you'd expect him to look like -- a marshmallow.

I kind of liked him -- he seemed real in a certain way, because he, like me, was an outsider.

But, it turned out he was nothing like that. He talked to me, pretended to be my friend, but then -- in the end -- when it came to talking to me in public or texting me or acknowledging me as a human being -- the minute he did not need me to share my homework with me, he was gone.

I can't let myself think about it too much even now. It hurts too much. I thought he really liked me, but he was just playing me for my homework.

Oh well. Stupid me.

I was probably saved from something hideous.

But, what was that hideous something he might have saved me from? Who knows...

In many ways, it just does not matter.

I just wish I could get my mother back.

CHAPTER TWENTY-THREE

The truth about my father comes in pieces, like a puzzle I'm assembling without knowing what the final picture should look like.

From Mom's wine-loose confessions: He was never good with money. He had "wandering eyes." He made promises he couldn't keep.

From overheard phone calls: He's not actually in Colombia. He's in Denver, working construction and living with a woman named Carla who has two kids of her own.

From the letters I'm not supposed to know about: He wants to see me, but Mom won't let him. He sends money because the court makes him, not because he wants to.

From my own heart: I miss him so much it feels like dying.

The day I finally get the courage to call him, using Gus's help to find his phone number, my hands shake so hard I can barely dial.

"Hello?" The voice is older than I remember, rougher, but definitely his.

"Dad? It's... it's Marie Elise."

Silence. Then: "Baby? Oh my God, baby, is that really you?"

And just like that, I'm four years old again, climbing into his lap while he reads me stories about brave princesses and magical kingdoms.

"I've been trying to call you for two years," he says, and his voice is thick with tears. "Your mother changed the number. She won't return my calls."

"She told me you didn't want to see me anymore."

"Want to see you? Sweetheart, you're the only thing I think about. I have pictures of you all over my apartment. I send birthday cards and Christmas presents, but I never know if you get them."

We talk for two hours. He tells me about his job, about Carla and her kids, about the studio apartment he keeps just for me if I ever want to visit. I tell him about school, about dance, about Mom's drinking and the pills and the man who's trying to steal from us.

"I'm coming to get you," he says immediately.

"You can't. Not yet. Mom needs help first, and I can't abandon the animals."

"You're nine years old, Marie. You shouldn't have to take care of your mother."

"But I do. And I can't leave the animals."

I tell him about my rescue operation, about the dozen creatures depending on me for survival. I expect him to tell me I'm being ridiculous, that I'm just a child playing pretend. Instead, he's quiet for a long moment.

"You know what?" he finally says. "I'm proud of you. You've got a bigger heart than anyone deserves."

When Dad finally comes to see us, six months after that first phone call, I almost don't recognize him. He's older, grayer, wearing jeans and work boots instead of the business suits I remember. But his eyes are the same blue-gray as mine, and when he sees me waiting on the front porch, he starts crying.

"You're so big," he says, holding me tight. "You're so grown up."

We talk for hours -- about his life in Denver, about why he left, about the mistakes he made and the guilt he carries. He tells me about Carla and her kids, about how he wants me to meet them someday but only if I want to.

"I'll never ask you to choose," he says. "I just want to be part of your life again, whatever that looks like."

Mom watches from the doorway, arms crossed, not quite ready to forgive but not actively hostile either. They have their own conversation later, one that ends with both of them crying and agreeing to try to co-parent better.

Dad can't move back -- too much has happened, too much trust has been broken. But he can visit every other weekend. He can call whenever I want. He can be present in the way he should have been all along.

CHAPTER TWENTY-FOUR

I never planned to become friends with Kithie Wexthrall. Friendship requires proximity and trust, and Kithie doesn't trust anyone. But sometimes life puts people in your path for reasons you don't understand until later.

It was a Thursday afternoon when I saw her sitting alone behind the school, her back against the brick wall, knees drawn up to her chest. She was crying -- not the dramatic sobbing that some girls do for attention, but the quiet, hopeless kind of crying that comes from somewhere deep and dark.

"Are you okay?" I asked, though it was obvious she wasn't.

She looked up at me with those storm-cloud eyes, and for a moment I thought she might tell me to go away. Instead, she said, "Do you ever feel like you're drowning, but everyone else is breathing just fine?"

I sat down beside her on the cold concrete. "Every day."

That's how I learned about the real incident that made her famous in all the wrong ways. The truth about Gus's NERF gun and pickleball paddles, about the panic and the handcuffs and the social media storm that followed.

"I tried to explain," Kithie told me that day behind the school. "I kept saying it wasn't mine, that I didn't even know it was there. But once that word gets out -- 'gun' -- nobody listens to the rest of the story."

"Are you angry at Gus?" I asked.

She was quiet for a long time. "I was. But he's just a kid, you know? He didn't mean for any of this to happen. And he felt so bad afterward, he cried for hours when he realized what had happened."

"They're sending me away," she tells me during one of our later conversations, when we're sitting on the broken moon bridge with our feet dangling over the edge.

"Where?"

"Some therapeutic boarding school in Utah. Mom says it's for my own good, but really it's because I'm bad for her image. Hard to get acting work when everyone knows your daughter is the school shooter girl."

"You're not a school shooter."

She looks at me then, and her storm-cloud eyes are full of a pain so deep I can barely stand to see it.

"How do you know? How does anyone know what I might do?"

"Because I know you. Because you feed the stray cats behind the 7-Eleven when you think no one is watching. Because you help little kids who get lost in the store. Because you're sitting here crying instead of planning revenge."

"Sometimes I want revenge," she whispers. "Sometimes I want to hurt everyone who's ever hurt me."

"That's normal. I want revenge too, sometimes."

"On who?"

I think about Chase Branch, about Mom's pills, about Dad's absence, about all the people who throw away animals like they're garbage.

"Everyone," I say.

We sit in comfortable silence, two damaged girls watching the sun set over a broken world. Finally, Kithie speaks again.

"If I have to go away, will you watch out for Gus? He acts tough, but he's really not."

"I will."

"And will you keep being friends with me? Even from far away?"

"Always."

Kithie does go away to Utah, but she comes back different. Calmer. Her edges are still sharp, but they're turned inward now instead of threatening to cut everyone else. She's learned to channel her darkness into art -- haunting, beautiful drawings that capture pain and transform it into something meaningful.

"I'm not cured," she tells me the day she returns. "There's no cure for being broken like this. But I've learned how to live with it."

She shows me her sketchbook -- pages and pages of creatures that are part human, part animal, part something else entirely. They're dark but not hopeless, complex but beautiful.

"I want to help," she says. "With your rescue operation. I think maybe helping other broken things might help me too."

CHAPTER TWENTY-FIVE

The breeze is dry, but wet with promise.

Entire blocks of memory and experience waver in my mind as I ride my bicycle to the studio.

My new friend is in her home.

Probably alone.

Her mother is working in her office. Her father is working at his second job.

The mortgage must be paid. They owe more than the house it worth, but neither the mom nor the dad wants to walk away.

So they work two jobs. They spend a lot of time away from home.

Probably alone.

The sun is still far from setting, the afternoon is dark, dark, darker -

Perception is uncertain...at least mine, at least these days.

My mother speaks incessantly of places that no longer exist; do we even live in the same universe? Our worlds converge not at all, except, perhaps, in the

but may no longer exist (?)

The Painted Desert (36th and Shartel in OKC?)

Alamo Courts Motel (Shartel, south of downtown OKC)

A Midi ... bottom of the parking garage, Liberty Bank, OKC

Liberty Bank

Women's Building Swimming Pool at the University of Oklahoma

Norman Library in the basement of the post office ?

Winchell's Donuts -- on Main Street near the Downtown Shopping Center

Gardski's Loft - Amarillo, TX -- an oasis of sorts -- beer and great nachos on a Friday night

Amarillo Town Club -- amazing 25-yr Jr Olympic reg pool

Cinema East movie theatre on East Alameda in Norman -- saw Harold and Maude and numerous other films there

Drive-in movies: two in Norman, now gone

Pick's Tamales in Paul's Valley? Wynnewood? Davis? Somewhere on highway 77, on the way to Ardmore

Sooner Tots and Teens -- cute boutique in downtown Norman with cute outfits for children

Peaches -- chain of stores selling music in Tulsa

Main Street Exercise Studio: exercise studio in Norman (24th and Main)

Marie Keeling's Dance Studio (ballet for girls) on Main Street in Norman

The bricks were painted a dark burgundy color, which made one wonder what the original color was. It was probably a dark orange, but that's only a guess. The neighborhood contained an uncomfortable blend of styles and functions. The gentrification, when it occurred, was spotty and sporadic. Gentrification just didn't take in any kind of uniform way, which was a bit inexplicable to many people who drove by.

Neko Sushi appeared to be in the midst of renovation. It was on the end of a one-story strip mall. On the end of the strip mall near the intersection, "Happy Times" Liquor glowed with green neon. A yellow arrow with black block letters, "LIQUOR STORE" was positioned on the edge of a white painted metal pole. The liquor store's plate glass windows were protected by metal bars. Next door, Daylight Donut offered false hope to anyone hoping for a breakfast consisting of anything but donuts and coffee. In the parking lot was a white Tundra pickup, a gray Honda Civic. Last week, they put in a new sidewalk across the street. The asphalt street was too narrow for the volume of traffic that traversed it, and there were numerous small potholes. The sign for Neko Sushi had been replaced. "Lucky's Bar & Grill & Sushi" in brown san serif type. The "L" was in the middle of a big circle, which gave it a bit of a bulls-eye appearance.

It takes almost a year, but I finally convince the owners of Neko Sushi to change their name. The new sign reads "Lucky Cat Sushi" in cheerful red letters, with a smiling maneki neko underneath.

Meridian and I celebrate by ordering takeout and eating it in the sunroom with the animals. Rusty the fox has brought his mate and three kits to live in the woods behind our house, and they sometimes come to the windows to watch us work.

"You did it," Meridian says, toasting me with a can of soda. "You actually changed something."

"We did it," I correct her. "All of us."

Gus has officially joined our rescue operation, using his tech skills to create a network of motion-activated cameras that help us find animals in need. Kithie volunteers on weekends, her gentle hands surprisingly good at coaxing frightened creatures to trust again. Even Mom helps, using her business skills to turn our informal rescue into a proper nonprofit organization.

CHAPTER TWENTY-SIX

In principle, I am against people having pets.

It's a kind of slavery, and it's tragic. The poor animal has no rights at all.

I'm not saying that all animals are mistreated. After all, a lot of people are closer to their pets than to members of their own family. My mom's Aunt Terrister has two dachshunds that she considered her little girls. She said she wants to be buried with them, but I think that's against the law. It's a rather grisly thought, but I think it has to do with health regulations.

On the other hand, some people need companion animals. They need a sounding board -- someone who will listen passively as they pontificate on politics.

But, what can you do?

This philosophical dilemma weighs on me as I continue my rescue work. Am I just creating a different kind of captivity? Are the animals I save truly free, or have I simply replaced one form of imprisonment with another?

I discuss this with Dorothy one evening as we're feeding the creek cats.

"Child," she says, settling her weathered hands on my shoulders, "there's a difference between saving a life and owning a life. You're not keeping these creatures because you want to possess them. You're healing them so they can choose their own path."

She gestures toward Rusty, who watches us from the edge of the woods, wild and free but choosing to stay near.

"That fox could leave anytime he wants. He stays because this place feels safe to him. That's not slavery -- that's sanctuary."

Maybe she's right. Maybe there's a difference between pet ownership and providing refuge. Maybe the animals understand the distinction even if I'm still working it out.

CHAPTER TWENTY-SEVEN

On my tenth birthday, Dad takes me to see the real Painted Desert in Arizona. It's a road trip -- just the two of us, camping under stars so bright they look like someone scattered diamonds across black velvet.

The desert is nothing like I expected. It's not brown and boring like I thought it would be. Instead, it's layers of red and purple and gold, carved by wind and water into impossible shapes that look like sculpture. It's harsh but beautiful, damaged but somehow made more beautiful by the damage.

"This is what healing looks like," Dad says as we watch the sunrise paint the rocks in shades of fire. "Not perfect. Not unmarked. But transformed."

I think about Mom, sober now for eight months and working again as a consultant. I think about Kithie, channeling her pain into art. I think about all the animals I've rescued, scarred but safe. I think about myself -- still small, still sharp-edged, but no longer alone.

"I want to come back here someday," I tell Dad.

"We will," he promises. "Every year, if you want."

Standing there in the painted desert, I finally understand what Mom meant about places that no longer exist. It's not that the places themselves are gone -- it's that we change, and our relationship to them changes, and sometimes the person who loved that place doesn't exist anymore.

But maybe that's okay. Maybe we're all painted desert -- carved by experience, made beautiful by the carving.

CHAPTER TWENTY-EIGHT

A year later, Chase Branch is arrested for fraud -- not for what he tried to do to us, but for scamming three other women in similar situations. The trial makes local news, and several more victims come forward. He gets five years in prison, which feels like justice, even if it came too late for some of his victims.

Kithie graduates from75 high school a year early and gets accepted to art school with a full scholarship. Her final project is a graphic novel about a girl who saves broken things -- animals, people, herself. The main character looks suspiciously like me, if I had dark hair and storm-cloud eyes.

"It's called 'The Painted Desert,'" she tells me, showing me the cover. "Because that's what you taught me -- that being broken doesn't mean you can't be beautiful."

Gus starts high school and immediately joins the robotics team, where his skills with computers and his gentle way with living things make him invaluable for building assistive devices for disabled animals. He's still small and still has unruly red curls, but he walks taller now, more confident in his own skin.

Meridian wins a national art contest with her wildlife drawings and gets a scholarship to summer art camp. Her parents are so proud they frame the acceptance letter and hang it in their living room next to her father's GED certificate and her mother's employee of the month awards.

Mom celebrates two years of sobriety by getting her consulting business fully re-established. She's different now -- steadier, more grounded, but also more compassionate. Her work now focuses on helping small nonprofits and community organizations, using her business skills to make the world a little bit better.

Dad visits every other weekend religiously, and I've met Carla and her kids. They're nice people, and while it's still awkward sometimes, we're building something that feels like family. He's talking about moving back to Oklahoma eventually, maybe buying a house close enough that I could walk between both homes.

CHAPTER TWENTY-NINE

On my twelfth birthday, we have a party in the sanctuary. It's not a typical kid's party -- instead of bounce houses and cake, we have an open house for the community to meet the animals and learn about wildlife rescue. Local news covers it, and by the end of the day, we have a waiting list of volunteers and enough donations to expand our operation.

I wear my hair down for the party, letting it flow loose around my shoulders instead of in my usual braids. I'm taller now, less sharp-edged, though my eyes are still serious and my smile still rare. But when I do smile -- really smile -- people notice.

As the sun sets and the last visitors leave, my chosen family gathers in the garden: Mom and Dad (still awkward with each other but trying), Dorothy and Miguel, Kithie and Gus and Meridian, even Elena Wexthrall who's been sober herself for six months and is slowly rebuilding her relationship with her children.

We sit around the fire pit Dad built, watching Rusty and his family emerge from the woods for their evening hunt. The foxes pause at the edge of the firelight, wild but unafraid, and I think about how far we've all come.

"Speech!" Gus calls out, and everyone laughs.

I stand up, feeling suddenly shy with all these eyes on me. But these are my people, my pack, my chosen family, and they deserve to know what they mean to me.

"Two years ago," I begin, "I thought I was saving animals. But really, they were saving me. All of you were saving me."

I look around the circle -- at Mom's clear eyes, at Dad's patient smile, at my friends who've become siblings, at the adults who've become mentors and protectors.

"I used to think that broken things couldn't be fixed," I continue. "But I was wrong. Broken things can heal. They just heal differently than things that were never broken. They heal stronger."

Rusty's kit, Scarlett, now fully grown and with kits of her own, emerges from the shadows and sits just outside the circle. She watches us with intelligent dark eyes, wild but trusting, free but connected.

"We're all painted desert," I say finally. "Carved by wind and weather and time, but made beautiful by the carving."

As if summoned by my words, a shooting star streaks across the sky above us. Everyone makes a wish -- I can see it in their faces, that moment of hope and possibility.

I don't need to make a wish. I'm living mine already.

EPILOGUE - FIVE YEARS LATER

I'm seventeen now, and some dreams change while others remain constant. I still dance, and I did eventually spend a summer at the Metropolitan Youth Ballet, but I came back home with new skills and renewed appreciation for the life I've built here.

Our wildlife sanctuary has grown into a regional center for animal rescue and rehabilitation. We work with veterinary schools and conservation groups, and last year we successfully reintroduced a family of orphaned bear cubs to the wild.

Mom and Dad remarried last spring in a small ceremony in our garden, surrounded by family and friends and several very well-behaved rescue animals. It's not the same marriage they had before -- it's better, built on honesty and shared experience and the knowledge that love is something you choose every day, not something that just happens to you.

Kithie is in her third year of art school, creating sculptures that are shown in galleries across the country. Her work is still dark, still beautiful, still transformative. We email every week and visit when we can.

Gus is a freshman at MIT, studying artificial intelligence with a focus on conservation applications. He sends me prototypes of his latest inventions -- tracking collars that monitor animal health, motion sensors that can distinguish between different species, apps that help wildlife rescuers coordinate their efforts.

Meridian got into the art school of her dreams and is majoring in scientific illustration. Her drawings now appear in textbooks and nature magazines, bringing the beauty of wildlife to people who might never see these creatures in person.

I'm applying to colleges myself now, looking for programs that combine environmental science with animal behavior. I want to be a wildlife biologist, I think, or maybe a veterinarian who specializes in wild animal rehabilitation. The details matter less than the goal: to keep helping creatures that can't help themselves.

Some things never change. I still find abandoned animals by Willow Creek. I still rescue them, heal them, release them when possible. I still dance like my life depends on it, still lose myself in movement and music and the pure joy of physical expression.

I still miss the father I had when I was small, the mother I had before she got sick, the family that existed before everything fell apart. But I've learned that grief and gratitude can exist in the same heart, that you can mourn what you lost while celebrating what you found.

On quiet evenings, when the sanctuary is peaceful and all the animals are fed and safe, I sometimes sit on the old moon bridge and watch the sunset paint the sky in impossible colors. The bridge has been repaired now -- the city finally allocated funds to fix the broken railings and missing steps. But I remember what it looked like before, dangerous and beautiful and somehow perfect in its imperfection.

I think about the scared nine-year-old I used to be, dancing alone in an empty garage, convinced she was invisible and unwanted. I wish I could tell her that she was never invisible, that she mattered more than she knew, that the pain she was carrying would eventually transform into something beautiful.

I think about all the creatures I've rescued over the years -- the foxes and raccoons and dogs and cats and birds and all the others. Some stayed, some left, some died despite our best efforts, some thrived beyond our wildest hopes. But all of them mattered. All of them changed me. All of them taught me something about resilience, about love, about the fierce determination it takes to survive in a world that doesn't always want you.

Tonight, as I write this, Scarlett's granddaughter is curled up on my desk, purring as I work. Three generations of foxes have been born in our sanctuary now, wild but trusting, free but connected to this place that saved their ancestors.

Outside my window, I can see Mom and Dad working in the garden together, planning next season's plantings. I can hear Meridian's laughter from the sunroom where she's teaching a drawing class to local kids. I can see the lights from Dorothy and Miguel's cabin by the creek, where they've lived officially for two years now as our sanctuary caretakers.

This is what healing looks like: not perfect, not unmarked, but transformed. We are all painted desert now, carved by experience but made more beautiful by the carving.

And in the morning, when the sun rises over our small corner of the world, I'll put on my dance clothes and my worn leather slippers, and I'll dance. Not because I have to, but because I can. Not to escape my life, but to celebrate it.

Because this is what I've learned: we save what we love, and we become what we save. We are wild things choosing to be gentle. We are broken things choosing to heal. We are lost things choosing to find our way home.

We are painted desert, and we are beautiful.

THE END

ABOUT THE AUTHOR

Susan Smith Nash, Ph.D., is a writer, scholar, and innovator whose work bridges science, philosophy, and the humanities. With a background in geology, resource economics, American, British, and Paraguayan literature, rhetorical theory, and instructional design, she brings a unique lens to speculative fiction. Her writing explores themes of consciousness, resilience, and transformation. Nash is the author of numerous books and articles, and she currently leads programs in emerging science and technology. Todos Santos is her latest work of literary science fiction.

THE PAINTED DESERT

By Susan Smith Nash

Meet Lulu: dancer, hacker, animal rescuer—and nine years old.

In a crumbling neighborhood full of secrets, Lulu wages quiet war against cruelty, abandonment, and lies. With sharp wit, fearless heart, and unstoppable curiosity, she's uncovering truths the adults won't face. A tender, subversive coming-of-age novel, The Painted Desert explores fractured families, forgotten animals, and the transformative power of imagination.

Sometimes the bravest voices are the smallest.